RUMPELSTILTSKIN

First published in the United States 1991 by
Dial Books for Young Readers
A Division of Penguin Books USA Inc.
375 Hudson Street
New York, New York 10014

Published in Great Britain 1990 by
A & C Black (Publishers) Ltd
Printed in Italy by Arnoldo Mondadori
First Edition
N
1 3 5 7 9 10 8 6 4 2

Library of Congress Cataloging in Publication Data
Sage, Alison. Rumpelstiltskin.
Summary: A strange little man helps the miller's
daughter spin straw into gold for the king on the
condition that she will give him her firstborn child.
[1. Fairy tales.   2. Folklore—Germany].
I. Spirin, Gennadii, ill.   II. Rumpelstilzchen
(Grimm version). English.   III. Title.
PZ8.S127Ru   1991   398.21'0943   [E]   90-3950
ISBN 0-8037-0908-0

RUMPELSTILTSKIN

by The Brothers Grimm · retold by Alison Sage
Paintings by GENNADY SPIRIN

 DIAL BOOKS FOR YOUNG READERS NEW YORK

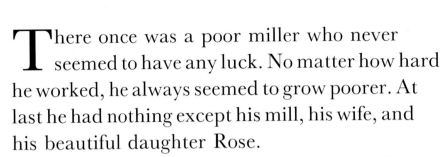

There once was a poor miller who never seemed to have any luck. No matter how hard he worked, he always seemed to grow poorer. At last he had nothing except his mill, his wife, and his beautiful daughter Rose.

"If the King thought you were somebody special," said his wife, "he would come to visit us. Then everyone would want to use our mill and we'd soon be rich."

"Don't be silly," said the miller, but his wife's words stuck in his mind and a daring plan came to him. Early the next morning he set off for the palace.

At the palace gates the miller asked to see the King. The King ordered the miller to be brought before him.

"Your Majesty," the miller began — and he trembled with fright as he spoke. "Your Majesty, my daughter can spin straw into gold."

"She can, can she?" said the King. "Bring her to the palace and we'll see. If what you say is true, then you'll be richly rewarded." He paused and frowned. "But if she fails, she'll lose her head."

This was not at all what the miller had expected.

"No, no…I made up the whole story!" he cried, but no one would listen. There was nothing left for him to do but go home and tell his daughter what the King had said.

Rose was horrified. "But what's done is done," she said. "The King may yet change his mind." And with that, she set out for the palace.

When the King saw lovely Rose, he was surprised at her grace and courage. But all he said was: "So here is our Goldenfingers! I have filled a room with straw for you. Before morning you must spin every scrap into gold — or lose your head."

Even the guards felt sorry for Rose as they locked her in the room at the top of the tower. How could anyone spin straw into gold?

Rose sat down by the spinning wheel and tears rolled down her cheeks.

"If there's one thing I hate, it's crying," said a voice at her elbow.

Startled, she looked down and saw a little man with a long gray beard.

"I beg your pardon," said Rose, "but who are you?"

"Never you mind," said the little man. "I know who *you* are and it would be a shame for you to lose that pretty little head. I might even help you, if you had something to give me in return."

Rose felt a sudden hope. "You can have my necklace," she said. "It belonged to my grandmother."

"Hmm, not much," said the little man, "but it'll do."

He sat down at the spinning wheel and — *whirr whirr whirr* — it went around so fast that all you could see was a blur and the flash of bright straw. Rose felt strangely sleepy as she watched him.

All of a sudden she heard the King opening the tower door. It was morning! Terrified, she leapt to her feet — and the room was full of glittering gold. Not one scrap of straw remained, and there was no sign of the little man.

The King was delighted but he did not show it. He wanted more gold.

"I have filled a second room with straw," he said. "If you spin every scrap into gold before sunrise, your father will have his reward. Otherwise, you'll lose your head."

Rose wept. This room was twice as big as the last one, but what did that matter? She could not spin even one piece of straw into gold.

"Still crying?" said a voice. It was the strange little man. "What will you give me this time to spin your straw into gold?"

Rose dried her tears as fast as she could. "My ring," she said. "It was given to me by my mother."

Exactly as before, the little man sat down at the spinning wheel and — *whirr whirr whirr* — exactly as before, Rose fell into a deep sleep. By the time the first rays of the morning sun slipped in through the tower window, the room was glistening with spun gold. But still the King wanted more.

"One more night you must spin straw into gold," he said. "If by sunrise not a scrap of straw remains, you shall become my wife. If you fail, you will lose your head."

He could not help hoping she would succeed. Where else would I find a wife richer or more beautiful? he thought.

Rose was locked in the tower for a third night, and the room was three times as big as before. Patiently she waited for the little man.

"What will you give me this time?" he asked as soon as he appeared.

"I have nothing left to give you," said Rose. "But if you take pity on me now, I'll give you anything you want when I am Queen."

"Anything, eh?" said the little man, his eyes glinting. "Then you must give me your firstborn child."

Poor Rose, what could she do but agree?

"Don't forget!" warned the little man. "We have made a bargain."

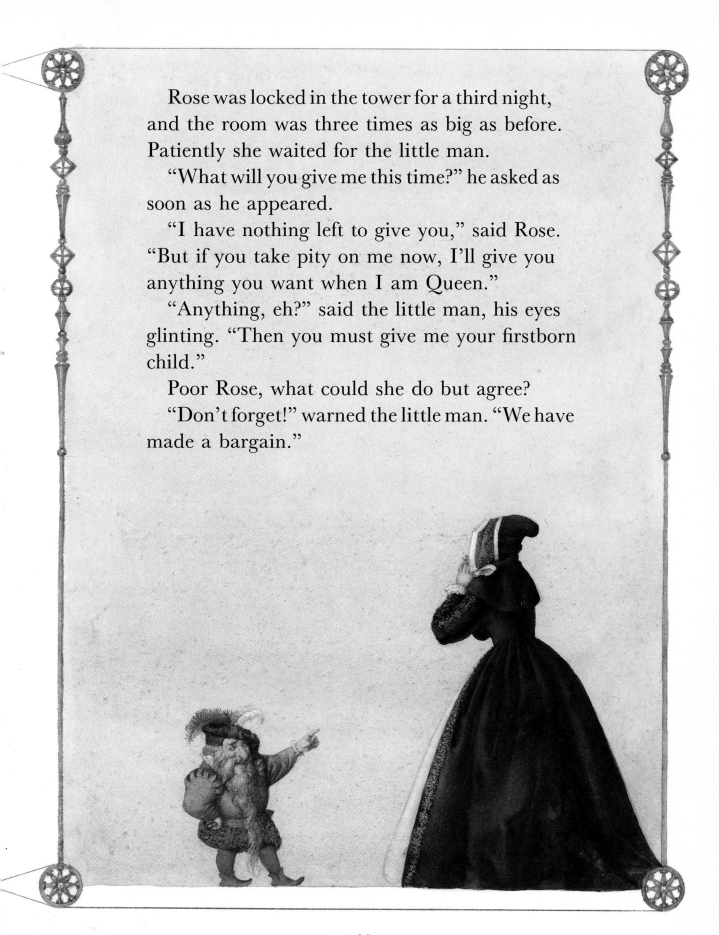

The King waited impatiently for the sun to rise.
As he opened the door of the tower room, he
blinked at the brilliance before him. The room
was filled to the rafters with gleaming gold.

Soon all the bells in the land were ringing for
the new Queen, and the miller and his wife cried
with joy to see their daughter such a fine lady.

Many months passed — and by the time that
Rose had a pretty little baby in her arms, she had
forgotten all about the little man and her promise
to him. But one day, almost a year later, she
heard a horribly familiar voice at her elbow.

"We have a bargain, my lady," said the little man. "That child is mine!"

In vain Rose wept and offered him gold and jewels.

"What do I need with gold?" he grinned, his eyes as cold and bright as a lizard's. "But I cannot bear crying. Guess my name, and you can keep your child. I'll give you three days, and three guesses on each day. If you can't" — he tossed his gray beard impudently — "then the baby's mine!"

Rose quickly sent messengers to ride to every corner of the land in search of names. First they found simple ones like Tom, Dick and Harry, James and John.

Then they brought in stranger ones like Wigglebottom and Curlytoes, Bundlewick and Chumpers. Rose's heart sank. How could she tell if any belonged to the little man?

At the end of the first day the little man
appeared as promised.

"My name, lady?" he demanded.

"Is it Andrew?" she faltered.

"No!"

"Is it Belshazzar?"

"No!"

"Is it Caspar?" she said, almost in tears.

"No, and you'll never guess it," he crowed.

The second night Rose cried and begged, but the little man seemed to feel no pity. At each wrong guess his eyes lit up in triumph. "One more night and the baby is mine!" he jeered.

The third day came and Rose shut herself in her room. One more day, she thought, and my happiness is gone for ever. Out of her window she could see the King as he set off hunting.

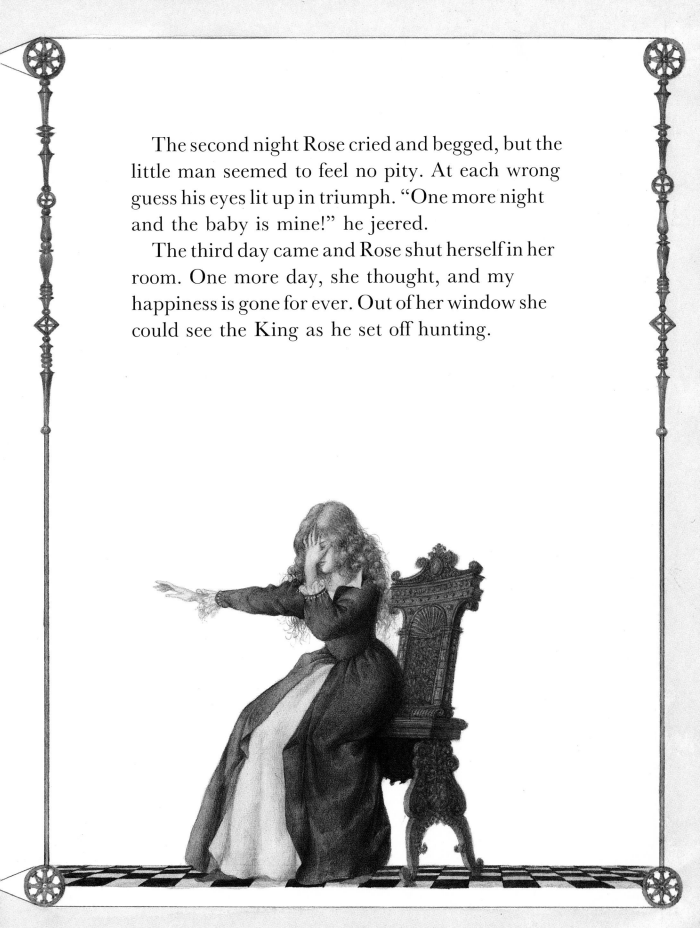

When the King came home from hunting that evening, he went in search of his wife.

"Rose, my love," he said, "I've just heard the strangest thing. Such a funny, squeaky little song and you'll never guess who was singing it."

"No," said Rose, not lifting her head.

"A little man with a long gray beard."

"A long gray beard?" cried Rose.

"Yes," said the King, glad to see the success of his story. "And he was spinning almost as well as you can. I could hardly see the wheel, it went around so fast. Let me see, what was he singing?

> *Nobody knows it*
> *Except him who chose it*
> *So I solemnly swear by the hair on my chin*
> *That my name it is: RUMPELSTILTSKIN!*

Joyfully the Queen kissed her husband. She could hardly wait for the little man to arrive.

That evening he appeared as suddenly as ever.

"I'll save you the trouble and take the child now," he said gleefully. "You won't guess my name."

"Is it Alfred?" said Rose.

"Nooo!"

"Is it Archibald?"

"Certainly not!"

Then Rose pointed at him, laughing, and began to sing…

Nobody knows it
Except him who chose it
So I solemnly swear by the hair on my chin
That my name it is: RUMPELSTILTSKIN!

The little man froze, unable to believe his ears. Then he flew into a towering rage. "Some witch told you that!" he shrieked.

"Be off with you," said Rose. "I've kept our bargain!"

The little man was now in a hideous fury. He stamped his foot so hard that it went through the floor. He struggled to free himself, and his beard became tangled in the splintered wood. At last with a frightful scream he vanished, leaving nothing but a few wisps of gray hair behind.

That night Rose smiled happily as she sang her baby to sleep. She knew that as long as she lived, she would never again see Rumpelstiltskin.

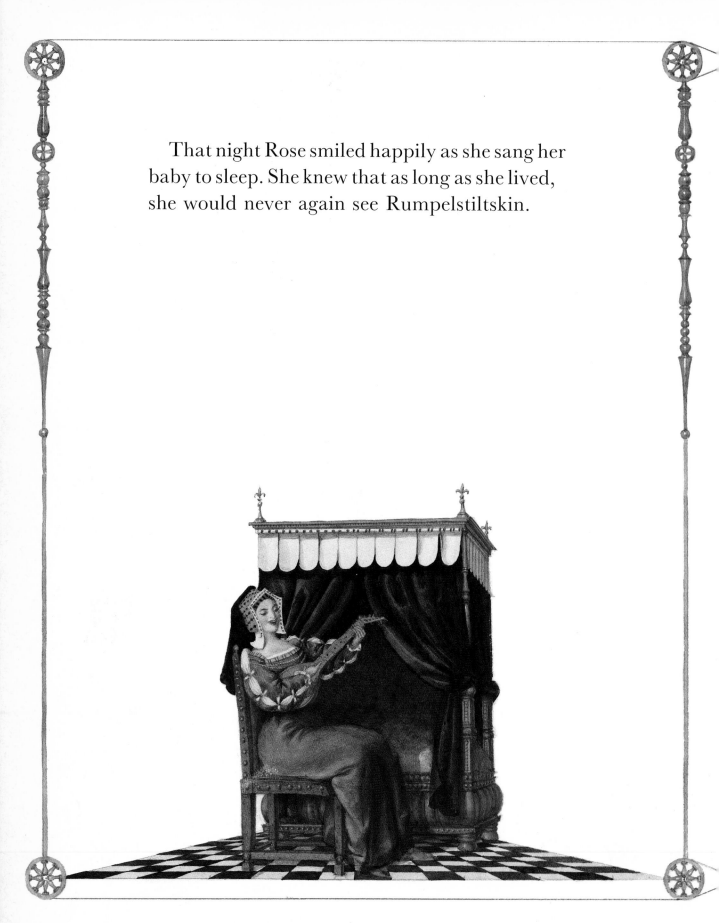

TENLEY